MARVEL

DOCTOR
STRANGE

THE JUNIOR NOVEL

Little, Brown and Company

Hachette Book Group
1290 Avenue of the Americas, New York, NY 10104
Visit us at lb-kids.com

Little, Brown and Company is a division of Hachette Book Group, Inc.
The Little, Brown name and logo are trademarks of Hachette Book Group, Inc.

The publisher is not responsible for websites (or their content) that are not owned by the publisher.

First Edition: October 2016

ISBN 978-0-316-27157-8

Library of Congress Control Number: 2016944727

10 9 8 7 6 5 4 3 2 1

LSC-C

Printed in the United States of America

33614057781147

MARVEL

DOCTOR STRANGE

THE JUNIOR NOVEL

BY STEVE BEHLING

Based on a Screenplay by Jon Spaihts, Scott Derrickson, C. Robert Cargill
Produced by Kevin Feige
Directed by Scott Derrickson

LITTLE, BROWN AND COMPANY
New York   Boston

CHAPTER 1

How did I get here?

We've all asked ourselves that question at one time or another. Usually, we're thinking about the decisions we've made, the events that led to one important, significant moment in our lives. It's almost a metaphysical question—how did we come to occupy this space, this moment in the universe? We might as well be asking, *Why am I here?*

Yeah, that's not what was running through

Stephen Strange's mind when he wondered, *How did I get here?*

What he really wanted to know was, how did he get to Greenwich Village? Like, physically. Because just a second ago, he was standing in an ancient library in an ancient place called Kamar-Taj, with his less-than-ancient colleagues Mordo and Wong.

Strange drew in a deep breath, and surveyed his surroundings. There was no mistaking it—this was New York City's Greenwich Village. Bleecker Street, to be specific. *(Thanks, street sign.)* The telltale brownstone apartment buildings and coffee shops were a familiar sight to Strange, who used to live in this place, the city that never sleeps.

That was before Kamar-Taj.

That was before the accident.

"You wanna maybe move sometime today?"

Strange whirled around to see an older man with a cane standing next to him. The wrinkled man scrunched up his nose and smacked his lips a few times. It was only then that Strange realized he was standing in the middle of a sidewalk and blocking the path of the older man. He quickly moved.

"Sorry, just getting my bearings," Strange said slowly.

"Eh, that's me every day," replied the older man. "Good luck with the circus." And the older man shuffled off down the sidewalk.

Circus? thought Strange. Then he remembered, looked down, and saw what the older man meant. He was still wearing the blue robes he had acquired in Kamar-Taj. The blue robes of a true disciple of The Ancient One. The flowing garment certainly set him apart from the other people walking the New York streets—the tourists, the local hipsters. These other people, by the way, were actively staring at Strange in his peculiar garb—peculiar even by New York standards, which is really saying something.

Whirling around again, Strange spied a three-story building behind him. A brownstone. Lifting his eyes, he saw a large, round window. Within the window, there was a peculiar curving lattice pattern. The pattern formed a symbol, one that Strange recognized.

It was the symbol of the Sanctum Sanctorum.

Strange rushed toward the building, raced up the steps, opened the door, and went inside.

CHAPTER

It would have been hard for Doctor Stephen Strange to separate this day from any other. It was nothing special. He found himself inside a scrub room at Metropolitan General Hospital, washing his hands and forearms. Another day, another operation.

He pulled on a pair of surgical gloves, releasing the elastic opening on his right wrist to produce a satisfying *snap*. The sound caused Strange to grin. He looked at himself in the mirror just above the scrub sink. What had gotten him here, to this moment in time? Hard work and a lot of natural talent. Strange took in the gray hair at his temples. *And experience.*

Let's do this, he said to himself.

"D octor Bruner," Strange said through his surgical mask as he strode into the operating room.

"Stephen," replied Bruner. Bruner was an anesthesiologist. She stood over the patient on the table, administering an anesthetic and monitoring the patient's vital signs.

Beneath his surgical mask, Strange smiled. "Are you flirting with me, Doctor Bruner?"

"Don't encourage him," came another voice,

that of Doctor Varma. "We can all barely fit in here with his ego as it is."

Strange smiled again, though Varma and Bruner couldn't see it because of the surgical mask. But his eyes crinkled at the corners, betraying his amusement.

"You wound me, Doctor Varma! Yesterday you said my ego could fill up this hospital. Now it's only a measly room?" Strange barely suppressed a chuckle, and he could practically hear the sound of Varma and Bruner rolling their eyes. Did they like Strange? Certainly. Did he have a large ego? Unquestionably.

Amid the camaraderie, a curious thing was happening. Strange and his colleagues had gone to work. The doctor with the ego large enough to fill a measly room, or possibly an entire hospital (given the day), moved his fingers almost imperceptibly. Delicately. Like a concert pianist.

Through a small hole they had made in the patient's scalp, Strange and Varma slid the endoscope. Its camera opened another world to Strange—he could see the patient's brain. Moving with grace and a practiced ease, Strange guided the endoscope until he found what he was after.

"And this would be our friend the tumor," Strange said. "Like most friends, this one has outworn its welcome."

The tool Strange was using was highly advanced. Bleeding edge. The probe was laser tipped, and Strange zapped the tumor with incredible precision. Bursts of heat targeted the growth, eating away at the cancerous mass. One careful burst. Then another.

"And that," began Strange, "is how you save a life before your coffee gets cold." Strange looked up from the patient, toward a window overlooking the operating room. Behind the window, a group of medical students watched in amazement as Strange, Varma, and Bruner performed their miracle. The students burst out clapping, as if they had just witnessed a feat of magic, some sleight of hand that they could not explain.

Allowing himself to enjoy the moment, Strange turned toward the students and bowed, just slightly.

That's when the door to the operating room burst open, revealing the bloodstained medical scrubs worn by Doctor Christine Palmer. She motioned to Strange, clutching a tablet computer under her arm.

"Better get this, Stephen," said Varma, taking note of the scene that was unfolding. "We'll close up for you."

Strange nodded and moved toward Christine

in one fluid motion. Varma slipped in and started
the closing procedure.

hat is it?"

"A GSW," Christine replied.

Gunshot wound.

The pair moved down the hospital hallway
as they exchanged questions for information.
Christine handed the tablet to Strange, who swiped
through medical charts with his right forefinger.

"Amazing you kept him alive," Strange
observed, shaking his head. It didn't look good.
At first blush, it appeared nothing could be done
for the patient. No possibility of survival. Strange
looked down at an X-ray, then frowned.

"I think I found the problem, Doctor Palmer. You left a bullet in his head."

Christine caught herself just as she was about to roll her eyes—she wouldn't take the bait. "It's impinging on the medulla. I needed a specialist. But Nic diagnosed brain death."

"Nic...Nic diagnosed brain death?" replied Strange. Nic was Doctor Nicodemus West, a fellow surgeon whom Strange held in not-so-high regard. Strange flipped through the charts once more, then stared at an MRI image. Something wasn't right. It didn't add up. He looked at Christine. Their eyes met. *Are you thinking what I'm thinking?*

They sprinted down the hall.

The hospital emergency room was a mess of people. Hospital emergency rooms always are. It took a moment for Strange and Christine to make their way toward the GSW patient. Hovering over the patient's bed was Nic West. The dark-haired surgeon looked serious as he prepared for a medical procedure with the help of some attending physicians.

Out of breath and in a rush, Strange gasped. "I need a craniotomy set in Trauma, stat!"

Christine stared at West and the other physicians. "What are you doing?" she asked.

"Organ harvest. He's a donor now," West said coolly.

"I didn't agree to that!" yelled Christine.

West sighed. "I don't need you to agree. We've already declared brain death."

Strange pushed right past West and the other

physicians, inserting himself between them and the patient. Strange didn't speak a word, but his body language said, *You're wrong, West, just like you're always wrong.*

"Get him prepped for a suboccipital craniotomy," said Strange. He was going to remove the bullet lodged in the patient's brain.

West stared at Strange like he was some kind of grandstanding lunatic. "I'm the doctor on call here, and I'm not about to let you operate on a dead man!"

Strange shoved the computer tablet with the X-ray into West's face. "What do you see?"

"A bullet," West replied wearily. "Of course there's a bullet."

Strange shook his head. "A perfect bullet. A perfect bullet that punched through bone," he began. "It should be deformed. It's not."

West stared at Strange, not getting it.

"That means it's been hardened," Strange continued. "You harden a bullet with antimony—a toxic metal. If the metal leaches into the cerebral spinal fluid—"

West's eyes lit up. "Rapid onset central nervous system shutdown."

"The patient's not dead, but he is dying," said Strange. He gave West a thin smile. "Still want to harvest his organs?"

With that, Strange set off, the patient being wheeled right behind him, for the operating room.

That's the good part," said Christine as she and Strange walked away from the patient's family. The operation had been successful—Strange had extracted the bullet, and the patient would make a full recovery. "And I guess the good part for you was humiliating Doctor West in the operating room. You didn't have to do that."

"I didn't have to save his patient, either," said Strange. "Sometimes I just can't help myself."

The pair walked down the hospital hallway, exhausted. Strange extended the fingers on each hand, moving them back and forth, as if they were sifting through sand.

"I could really use you as my neurosurgeon on call," Christine said. "You could make such a difference."

Strange looked at Christine, then shook his head. "I'm fusing transected spinal cords. Stimulating neurogenesis in the central nervous system. The techniques I'm developing will save thousands of people for years to come. In the ER, you save what? That one guy?"

Christine looked at Strange. Her heart sank a bit, and she felt a heaviness as she stared at her friend. "You're right. In the ER, we only save lives. There's no fame, no TV interviews."

They had been over this territory before, had had the same conversation. Sure, the words were always different, but each side kept making the same points. Christine wanted Strange to use his gifts to help people however he could. Strange wanted to use his gifts...however Strange wanted to use them.

Changing the subject, Strange turned to Christine. "I have a presentation at the Neurological Society tonight, if you'd like to come."

Christine smiled. "Another speaking engagement. How romantic. I'll pass."

"We used to have fun going to these things together," Strange said a little sadly.

"*You* used to have fun. They weren't about *us*; they were about *you*," Christine replied, brushing back her hair.

"They weren't *only* about me."

Without skipping a beat, Christine said, "Stephen, *everything* is about you."

With that, she was gone, leaving Strange to his thoughts.

CHAPTER

3

As Stephen Strange stepped inside the foyer of the Sanctum Sanctorum, he noticed an eerie stillness. A quiet beyond quiet. A feeling of being frozen in time, like he was walking into a painting. Only *he* was in motion, only *he* caused sound. It was like nothing he had ever experienced before.

The foyer led to an ornate grand staircase. Strange hurried up the stairs, taking note of the sound of his feet, of his breathing. At the top of the stairs, he came to a large circular room, a rotunda. Inside were three enormous panoramic paintings. No, they weren't paintings—they were windows.

One window looked over a misty forest, trees as far as Strange's eyes could see. Another opened onto a spectacular view of a tempest-tossed ocean, the seas roiling in anger. The last window bore witness to isolated, snowcapped mountains.

I wonder what you'd pay for a New York apartment with these kinds of views, Strange thought, allowing himself a slight laugh.

Curiosity welling up within him, Strange opened the middle window, the one with the ocean view. For the first time since entering the Sanctum, Strange heard a sound that he did not make. It was the sound of the ocean itself, the crashing waves, the wind. He felt a spray of cool salt water on his face. This was no illusion; this was real. The window really did, somehow, open to the ocean.

"Gateways," Strange said aloud to himself. "These windows are gateways...portals to other parts of the world."

He looked about excitedly, until his eyes came to rest on something in the window's frame. It looked like some kind of control panel. Placing his hand on the controls, Strange turned a dial. The view inside the window changed abruptly—in the blink of an eye, the ocean was replaced by a vast, arid desert.

Strange was accustomed to being astonished these days. Ever since the accident. Ever since Kamar-Taj. Ever since The Ancient One.

Turning his attention from the mysterious gateways, Strange continued his exploration of the Sanctum. Right off the rotunda was another room, dark-colored. It had the feeling of an old museum or library, and yet, there was something quite modern about the design.

Lining the walls, he saw what could only be described as artifacts, relics of a time gone by. There were swords, daggers, and helmets. There were amulets of all shapes. Chalices and cauldrons of varying sizes.

"The Chamber of Relics," Strange said.

His mind raced as he lost himself in his thoughts. *How did I get here?*

The solitary moment came to an end with a sound. A sound not from within the Sanctum, but from without.

The sound of door chimes.

The sound shocked Strange back to reality, back to the moments just before he suddenly appeared on the streets of New York City.

"Kaecilius," he whispered.

CHAPTER

4

TIME WILL TELL HOW MUCH I LOVE YOU.

The words inscribed on the back of Stephen Strange's watch bored themselves into his mind. He glanced at the hands on the timepiece, and then at his own delicate surgeon's hands, clasping the black leather-covered steering wheel. His sports car was speeding along Manhattan's West Side Highway, ducking in and out of traffic, making its way north.

There was a time when Christine would have

gone with him to an event like this. The Neurological Society shindig would be a bore without her. Why did he keep pushing her away? Why did he push *everyone* away?

Strange tugged at the black bow tie he wore around his neck, fidgeting slightly in his tuxedo. He was tired of thinking about times past. Glancing down, he touched the controls for the car's satellite radio, the music breaking the silence. It was nothing Strange wanted to hear.

"No. No. No," said Strange, flipping through the channels, trying to find something that didn't hit his ears the wrong way. He finally heard a distorted guitar coming through a messed-up amplifier, signaling the start of a classic garage-rock song. Satisfied, Strange hit the gas pedal, and the car raced up the Henry Hudson Parkway, then made the turn onto the George Washington Bridge.

The afternoon gave way to early evening, and along with it came darkness. Strange was well on his way to the Neurological Society gathering, his sports car zooming along a lonely mountain highway outside New York City. To his left, a sheer cliff—he was high up, no doubt about that. Taking in the view, Strange continued on his way, driving as fast as his car would take him.

He tried to silence the thoughts in his head with another song, but it wasn't working. Not tonight. There was too much going on in his mind: Christine.

"Time will tell how much I—"

Before Strange could finish his sentence, he was interrupted by the ringing of his cell phone. The fingers of his right hand quickly turned down the volume of the car stereo, then danced across the console to the button that set his phone to speaker mode.

"Go ahead, caller one, you're on the line," said Strange.

"A thirty-five-year-old marine colonel, paralyzed," said the young voice on the phone. It was Claire, Strange's assistant. "Crushed his lower spine in some kind of experimental armor. Mid-thoracic burst fracture."

Strange divided his attention between driving and talking, giving each task just enough notice to be dangerous.

"I could help him," Strange said with a sigh. "So could fifty other guys. Come on, Claire. Give me something worth my time! I believe in you!"

Then it was Claire's turn to sigh, clearly

flustered. In the background, the song ended, and Strange shunted his attention away from driving and talking to finding the next perfect song. As his car thundered down the highway, Strange came upon a slow-moving vehicle. He flicked the wheel to the left, stepping on the gas, ready to pass.

And he would have, except for a new car that suddenly appeared right in front of him. Strange downshifted, slammed on the brakes, and moved back into his own lane, behind the slow-moving vehicle. Just in time. A second later, and Strange would have found himself in the ironic position of needing a doctor.

"Twenty-year-old female with an electronic implant in her brain to control schizophrenia. Struck by lightning," said Claire.

"Send me the—"

DING!

Claire knew her boss, and the second he asked her to send anything, she did exactly that. Strange's eyes darted down to his cell phone, where he saw a new text message and a photo. An MRI picture.

Rain started slowly hitting the windshield. In between driving and talking and finding a song and checking the MRI picture, Strange turned on the car's windshield wipers.

"MRI, got it ... so, the lightning cauterized the brain around the—"

The slow-moving car in front of Strange seemed to be moving even slower.

Why wasn't there a good song anywhere to be found?

Drop. Drop. Drop.

"Is the implant still operational?" asked Strange as he tried to make his way around the slow-moving vehicle yet again. Shifting into the opposite lane, Strange floored the gas pedal, pulling ahead. There was the sound of the phone and the music and the rain and the driving. As Strange swerved back into his lane, he heard a new sound. The screech of metal on metal.

His sports car hitting a slow-moving vehicle.

Strange skidded into a signpost, spun out of control and through a guardrail, and then plunged off the lonely mountain road.

CHAPTER

The door chimes rang in Strange's ears. *Time will tell*, he thought as he made a hasty exit from the Chamber of Relics, through the hallway, and past the rotunda, stopping at the top of the grand staircase.

This building, the Sanctum Sanctorum, was not his home. Yet Strange now found himself in the bizarre position of playing host to what he knew would be exceedingly unwelcome guests. Unlike a brain tumor, these guests would not be easily removed with a simple surgical procedure.

"Kaecilius," he whispered again.

The door chimes continued to resonate throughout the Sanctum. That's when Strange noticed it. It was subtle at first; he would have missed it had his keen eyes not been paying attention to every detail. The front door of the Sanctum appeared to shudder, then move, slightly inside, toward the foyer. It wasn't like a bulldozer slammed into the front of the building and started to drive it forward. No, the door moved like melted butter, sliding, shifting.

Three robe-clad figures slipped around the door and suddenly appeared in the foyer. It wasn't possible, and yet, it happened. Strange was used to the impossible these days.

He recognized the robes immediately. They were the same robes worn by all the denizens of Kamar-Taj, like Strange himself.

One of the robed figures looked impossibly strong, very much the "muscle" of the small group. Another one of the group, a woman with blond hair, looked around the foyer with a cruel sneer on her lips. Her gaze met that of the final robed figure, whose brown eyes came to settle on Strange.

After what seemed like an eternity of silence, the figure spoke. "How long have you been at Kamar-Taj, Mister . . . ?"

"Doctor," Strange responded instinctively.

The figure clad in the brown robe cocked his head and continued. "Mister *Doctor*?"

"It's Strange."

"Yes, but who am I to judge?" the robe-clad figure said, and then, with lightning-quick glances, silently ordered his comrades to attack. He smirked as they started to move.

It was all a blur to Stephen Strange.

CHAPTER

It was all a blur to Stephen Strange.

All of it—from the moment Strange's sports car collided with the slow-moving vehicle and spun out of control to the second it sliced through the guardrail and sailed over the cliff—was a blur. The sports car fell at least twenty-five feet before it hit the ground below and rolled. As it tumbled, its occupant was buffeted about, his senses reeling.

The car had built up so much momentum

that it continued to roll, smashing along the ground and crashing through a metal security fence. Strange saw it all unfold before his eyes, but it was like watching something that had already happened. Each moment of time was like a snapshot, a frozen image embedded in his panicking mind.

In the darkness, a metal post destroyed the windshield, shattering the safety glass. The front of the car was mangled as the vehicle at last came to rest in the dark river below. Water rushed in through the broken window.

Another frozen moment in time, watching the water pour in over his lower body.

Another snapshot—blood, everywhere.

He couldn't feel his hands. Where were his hands?

Strange was confused.

Time will tell. . . .

Water, cold.

My hands?

Darkness.

CHAPTER

7

They moved across the foyer of the Sanctum Sanctorum like encroaching darkness. Before Stephen Strange could react, two of the robed figures launched themselves at him, racing toward him at the top of the staircase. It was all happening so fast that Strange had barely enough time to notice that his robed assailants were not running up the stairs but the walls.

Up the walls.

This, Strange said to himself, *is* not *going to be easy.*

Strange made very deliberate hand gestures, slashing through the air. From nowhere, a luminous tendril of crackling energy appeared. Strange clasped it in his hand, like a whip. He cracked the energy whip at the robed woman, the one who was now closest to him. The air sizzled as the whip wrapped itself around the woman's legs.

Not just a woman, Strange remembered. *A Zealot.* It was coming back to him now. Wong and Mordo had told him about Kaecilius and the Zealots. They were members of The Ancient One's brood who had rebelled against the teachings of Kamar-Taj. They wanted power and eternal life. They absolutely did not see all life as precious, something to be protected at all costs.

With great effort, Strange yanked on the

luminous whip, sending the Zealot crashing away from him. Flicking the whip out once more, he snared a large ornamental vase, and then hurled it at the big Zealot, the strong-looking one. The Zealot was staggered by the shattering vase, but nothing more.

If I'm going to gain any ground here, I'm going to have to do a lot better than this.

As though reading Stephen's mind—and agreeing—Kaecilius smirked from where he stood in the foyer and, with a gesture, sent shards of energy hurtling Strange's way. Thinking quickly, Strange snapped the energy whip around him, deflecting the shards. It was messy, but effective. *Lucky,* Strange thought. *I got lucky.*

A quick scan of the situation showed the two Zealots were recovering from Strange's assault, and Kaecilius was rapidly approaching the stairs.

With no time to lose, Strange scrambled to his feet and sprinted down a corridor toward a hallway. He needed time. Time to formulate a plan. He moved down the hallway, toward the door at the end. He ran and ran and...

Was it him, or did the end of the hallway just get farther away?

Was the floor suddenly...moving...snaking...twisting?

Strange had a queasy sensation, as if all the input his senses were receiving was corrupt. It completely disoriented him. Focusing, he bolted for the end of the hallway. Again: queasiness. The harder he ran, the farther away the door seemed to be, and the more the floor seemed to shift beneath his feet. It was like being inside a carnival fun house, Strange mused—minus the fun.

He heard laughter.

"This really is as fun as it looks." Kaecilius cackled, as if reading Strange's mind once more.

Of course. Kaecilius was using his powers to warp reality. Strange should have realized this immediately. "Rookie mistake," Strange muttered under his breath. Drawing a deep breath, Strange centered himself, as he had been taught to do in Kamar-Taj. He was in control of his own reality.

Turning around to face his foe, Strange cleaved the air around him with his hands, his fingers moving subtly, almost imperceptibly, in specific patterns. Energy crackled around his palms, forming what looked like shields of energy.

"Fun's over," Strange said to Kaecilius, ready for whatever this madman and his Zealots had in store for him.

That's when the first of Strange's two energy shields flickered, then disappeared.

CHAPTER

First there was darkness and silence, nothing, like existence had just disappeared. A void. Like everything had ceased to be.

Then he saw a pinprick of light. Was it light? It was hard to tell. Slowly, the pinprick began to expand, and the light grew brighter and brighter. Then there was sound. White noise. Voices? Definitely voices, but distant.

Where was he? *When* was he? Was he in the

car? He was driving, yes? It was dark. Raining. He remembered that much.

The light grew brighter. Time was crawling.

"Stephen?"

Strange's eyes snapped open, and time suddenly resumed its regular shape. Bright lights shone on all sides of him, but it was hard for Strange to focus. Everything was blurry. There was so much activity around him, people, moving quickly. The sounds of machinery. Hospital machinery.

He was in a hospital.

"You've been in an accident."

He was the patient.

Trying desperately to focus his eyes, Strange saw Christine standing above him. She regarded him with a concern that Strange felt he didn't deserve.

"We've got you stabilized, but you're going into surgery," Christine said, her voice quivering with worry.

"Surgery? For what?" Strange tried to shout, but the oxygen mask strapped across his face prevented that. His lips moved, and what came out wasn't speech, but unformed sounds.

"Nic will take good care of you."

That's when Strange saw Doctor Nic West standing over him, next to Christine. West smiled. Strange didn't. His eyes went wide. He couldn't believe it. *Anyone* but Nic West.

"Don't worry, old man," West said comfortingly. "We'll save your hands."

"My *what*?" Strange tried to say, but again, only unformed sounds came out. Strange struggled to shift his head, moving so he could see his hands.

He did so with great difficulty, bucking against restraints, cutting through the fog of anesthesia. He looked down. He couldn't see his hands.

What he saw instead was layer upon layer of gauze wrapped around each hand. They didn't even look like hands; they looked more like clubs. The clubs were wet and stained red. Blood. Water.

Water rushing in through the broken window.

The car coming to rest in a dark river.

Sailing off the cliff.

Colliding with the slow-moving vehicle.

The accident.

Strange remembered.

Strange was moving. Wait—not in the car. Not anymore. He was back in the hospital on a gurney. The gurney was being wheeled down a hallway. Christine was there when Strange came to the doors of the operating room. West and

his team wheeled Strange in as Strange shouted,
"No! No! No!"

But all that came out were the same unformed
sounds as before.

Anesthesia. Then darkness.

Strange heard the sound of a loud breath
being drawn, and awoke with a start to
find that he was the one doing the breathing. He
looked around. He was still in the hospital. It was
still bright. But not like before. He was in a room:
a patient's room. There was a window, letting in
the morning sun.

My hands, Strange thought.

Looking down, Strange saw his hands before
him, wrapped in bandages. Between some of the

bandages, he could see bits of skin peeking out, black sutures dotting the landscape. His hands were suspended by a metal frame, so he could not move them. From what he could tell, his fingers were completely immobile—locked in place by surgical screws.

"It's gonna be okay."

Christine.

She was now standing next to his bed. She must have stayed with him while he was unconscious.

"What," began Strange, speaking with great difficulty, "did they do?"

Christine frowned, shaking her head. "They rushed you in by chopper, but it took a while to find you. The golden hours for nerve damage went by while you were still in the car."

"What," yelled Strange, fuming now, *"did they do?"*

Christine stared at Strange, her lips twitching, as she slowly moved her hands to her mouth. He wanted the truth, however ugly and hopeless. The truth.

"Eleven stainless-steel pins in the bones," she said, her voice quivering. "Multiple torn ligaments. Severe nerve damage in both hands. Nic did everything he could to—"

"*Nic?*" Strange rasped.

However ugly and hopeless.

The truth.

The truth? It was over. Life was over. Everything he had known before, everything he had worked for, gone forever. It had all vanished the moment his car went over the cliff and crashed into the murky water below.

"He worked on you for eleven hours...."

Strange wasn't listening. He was just staring

at his hands. His hands? Were these *things* really his hands now?

"No one could have done better—"

"*I'd* have done better," Strange shot back, his voice bitter and resentful.

Christine looked down, nodded, and took a deep breath. She tilted her head, gazing right at Strange.

"I'm sorry," she said, her voice cracking. "You weren't available."

Christine placed a hand on his shoulder. Strange stared right past her at the wall. Through the wall.

At nothing.

CHAPTER

It disappeared like nothing. Like it never existed.

The energy shield that had formed around Strange's hand was gone and, with it, his hope. Strange snapped his arms, remembering his training, trying to get the shield back. Energy flickered, and then faded.

It was no use.

Rookie mistake.

Through the twisting, turning, warping hallway,

Kaecilius reached Strange. With ease, he flipped Strange upside down and onto the ceiling. *Which way is up?* Strange thought, desperately trying to get his bearings.

From the corner of his eye, he caught Kaecilius smirking as the Zealots moved along the walls... or was it the floor? The ceiling? Strange could no longer tell. All he could do was brace himself for the assault to come.

Kaecilius waved a hand, summoning shards from thin air that hurtled toward Strange. With his remaining energy shield, Strange blocked the shards. But a sliver sliced through his tunic.

Blood. Wet. Water.

The accident.

One of the Zealots, the strong one, sensed Strange's lack of focus. He came after Strange. Using the luminous whip, Strange lashed out at the Zealot, keeping him at bay. Or mostly at bay. The Zealot connected with a blow of his own, sending Strange staggering backward.

Another attack. The other Zealot, the woman. Her anger and her rage were focused on him. Strange recoiled, trying to blunt the Zealot's energy shards. His shield was weakening and he was moving slower. *I'm fighting their battle*, Strange realized. *And I'm losing.*

Along with the battle, Strange was losing his senses once again. Reality seemed to melt around him. The strong Zealot gestured, and suddenly Strange found himself out of control, banging against the floor (was it the floor?), the ceiling (was it the ceiling?), and the walls (were they the walls?).

Battered, bruised, bloodied, Strange took a deep breath and focused himself. He saw Kaecilius waiting, watching. The strong Zealot, ready to attack. And at the very end of the hallway, which was now the floor, the blond Zealot. Behind her, Strange saw the rotunda.

The gateways, Strange thought.

He let himself fall.

CHAPTER

10

Falling asleep was impossible, yet staying awake was agony. There was no peace for Stephen Strange, lying in a hospital bed. The world around him was swirling, real and unreal. His life, the one he had known for years, had come to an end.

What day was it? Was it even daytime? Strange had been in the hospital so long, he could no longer tell the difference between the antiseptic hospital lighting and the sun. He had been in and out of surgery so much. The things that were his hands throbbed.

Strange slowly shifted his eyes downward, toward his hands, resting atop his blanket. Gone were the metal screws and apparatus that had kept them suspended in the air. They were now splinted with thermoplastic, keeping them in one position, to heal.

Strange laughed bitterly.

His hands throbbed. They always throbbed. The slightest movement of a finger caused excruciating pain. The hands that had moved with a grace to be envied, that had worked miracles, were now blunt instruments that brought Stephen Strange nothing but misery.

There was a rustling. Strange looked up, and it was only then that he noticed Christine had been sitting with him the whole time.

Was it day? Was it night? Night, maybe.

When am I? Strange thought.

He was sitting up in his hospital bed, a tablet computer propped before him on his lap. With enormous effort, he swiped at the touch screen, attempting to flick from one page to another. He winced at the pain. Watching his fingers try to activate the screen was like watching someone trying to thread a needle with a baseball bat. The action required finesse, but all Strange could do was bang a finger against the screen. He had no control.

Through gritted teeth, he studied the images on the tablet. X-rays. MRI images. Of the things that used to be his hands.

It was day. Strange knew that. At least he knew that. And it was *the* day—the day that the bandages would come off. The day he would finally know.

As he sat up in his bed, Doctor West and Doctor Varma stood beside him. They watched, scarcely breathing, as Christine slowly began to unwrap the bandages.

Strange was nervous. Frightened. Feelings he wasn't used to, feelings he didn't like.

The bandages continued to unravel. Strange gasped. Did it hurt? Was it phantom pain? Was it his mind? Was there a difference?

At last, the bandages were off.

"No."

"You've been in splints for months," West offered. "Give your body time."

The hands that Stephen Strange saw were not his, he was sure of it. They couldn't be; it was an impossibility. *These* hands were a lattice of angry red scars. He raised the hands that weren't his, and watched, helpless, as they shook.

The room was silent as Strange turned his gaze on West, then to Varma. Then, at last, to Christine.

"You've ruined me," he spat.

No one said anything.

Strange stared at nothing.

Weeks had passed since the accident. Months. Maybe years? Strange could no longer tell how long it had been. Time had ceased to mean anything. He was no longer a surgeon, he had nowhere to be, and he had nowhere to go. Nowhere. That's exactly where he was.

"Squeeze my hand now. . . . Harder. Show me your strength."

Strange looked up at the physical therapist. He was a big guy, burly. The kind of person who could snap you in two, the kind of person you tried to keep on their good side.

Where was he? *When* was he? Physical therapy. That's right. He had been out of the hospital for some time. He stared at the fluorescent light above, the chipped paint on the walls. The old steel furniture.

Strange nodded, then gasped as he tried to squeeze the therapist's hand. The muscles in his face twitched, and sweat formed at his shaggy hairline, trickling down toward his untrimmed beard.

He might as well not have bothered to squeeze at all.

"This is useless," he said, dejected.

"It's not useless," the therapist responded. "You can do this."

Strange rolled his eyes in frustration. "Right. Let me ask you, Bachelor's Degree: Have you ever known anyone with nerve damage this extensive to 'do this' and actually recover?"

Strange gestured with his head toward the angry red scars. They had faded somewhat, but the hands that weren't his still shook. They had a perpetual tremor. The therapist massaged Strange's hands and fingers, working along the joints. He cocked his head, pondering Strange's question. Then he gave a slow nod.

"One," he said.

Now it was Strange's turn to cock his head. He looked at the therapist. Not through him, but *at* him.

"Factory accident," the therapist began. "Broke his back. Paralyzed. His legs wasted away. Had pain from his wheelchair. Came in three times a week. Then one day he stopped coming. I thought he died."

Strange listened, enraptured.

"A few years later, he walked past me on the street."

"Walked?" Strange said, incredulous.

"Yeah, *walked*."

Strange's mind raced, like it did when he was performing neurosurgery, or searching for a song on satellite radio, or impatiently passing a slow-moving vehicle.

"What was the patient's name?" Strange asked.

"Pangborn, I think," said the therapist.

"Pangborn," Strange said aloud. *Not Jonathan Pangborn?* he thought.

Ⅰt was bright out in New York City, and a haggard, humbled Stephen Strange staggered along the street until he came to a basketball court. A group of men were playing. Strange had been waiting and watching for weeks, and now he spotted someone he recognized. The person he wanted to see, needed to see.

"Jonathan Pangborn," Strange said as he approached one of the basketball players. A man spun around, tall, erect. He stared at Strange, uncomfortable.

"You were a C-seven-C-eight spinal-cord injury. Complete."

The man looked around at his fellow players. He stepped away, and Strange followed. He stared at Strange. "Who are you?" he said.

"You were paralyzed," Strange continued, ignoring him. "Mid-chest down. Partial paralysis in both hands."

"I don't know you," said the man abruptly.

Strange tried to tone down his intensity. "My name's Stephen Strange. I'm a surgeon. I *was* a surgeon. But..."

Strange shrugged as he pulled his useless hands from the pockets of his shabby overcoat. He raised them to eye level, and the man watched them shake uncontrollably.

Jonathan Pangborn stared at Strange, a pitiful stare.

"Actually, I do know you. I came to your office," Pangborn said. "I never got past your assistant."

"You were untreatable."

"No glory for you in that, right?"

Strange looked away and took a breath. "Yet you came back from a place there's no way back from," Strange said quietly. "I...I'm trying to find my own way back."

From nothing, Strange thought. *From the nothing I have now.*

He thought of Christine.

Pangborn considered Strange, meeting his gaze. Behind them the basketball game was about to resume. The players waved at Pangborn to join them, but he dismissed them with a wave in return and walked with Strange.

"I'd given up on my body," Pangborn

whispered. "I thought, *My mind's all I have left. Let me at least elevate that.*"

Sounds familiar, Strange thought.

"I sat with gurus and wise women. Strangers carried me up mountains to see holy men. And finally I found my teacher in an unexpected place. And my mind *was* elevated, and my spirit deepened, and unexpectedly—"

"Your body was healed," Strange said, completing Pangborn's sentence.

Pangborn nodded. "There were deeper secrets to learn there. But I didn't have the strength to receive them. There were lessons, obligations... truths I wasn't ready for. So I chose to settle for my miracle and go home." His tone was wistful, sad.

For a moment, there was silence.

"The place you're looking for is called Kamar-Taj. But the cost there is high. Higher than you think."

"How much?" asked Strange.

"I'm not talking about money. That's all I can tell you. It's more than I should," Pangborn said, then turned back to the basketball game, walking away slowly.

Strange stared as the man who shouldn't—*couldn't*—be walking away did exactly that.

"Good luck," said Pangborn over his shoulder.

Strange would pay any price. Because his alternative was *this*.

Nothing.

CHAPTER 11

He let himself fall toward the rotunda, toward the robed Zealot who was waiting to annihilate him. With the agility ingrained in him by his martial-arts training at Kamar-Taj, Stephen Strange slammed into the woman, feet-first. The impact knocked her off-balance, and she fell into the rotunda.

The rotunda, with all its gateway windows.

For the first time since this all started, Strange allowed himself a tiny smile. The Sanctum

Sanctorum was full of surprises. Perhaps they would now work in Strange's favor.

The woman tumbled backward, through one of the gateway windows, shattering its glass outward in all directions. Strange evaded the broken glass as best he could, turning his gaze toward the gateway window.

It was like watching someone fall into a painting of a vast desert, barren and burning hot. Strange regained his footing as he saw the woman continue to tumble down a sand dune, disoriented.

Realizing what had happened to her, the Zealot struggled to make her way up the sandy slope, to no avail—her fingers and feet could find no purchase. She clawed at the grains of sand. Was she glaring at him? Strange wasn't sure if the Zealot could see back through the gateway and into the rotunda, the way he could still see her.

At that moment, he didn't care. His eyes caught the control pad on the gateway wall, and he knew what he had to do. With the swipe of a hand, Strange spun the dial, and where once there had been an arid desert, there was now a lush green forest, consumed by a midsummer's downpour. Rain sprayed through the shattered gateway window.

One down, Strange said to himself. *Two to—*

A bellow cut Strange's thought short, a nightmarish sound full of rage and sinister intent. The strong Zealot hurled himself at Strange. Crouching, the doctor remembered what Mordo had taught him. The moment the Zealot came into contact with his body, Strange moved with the Zealot, using his opponent's momentum against him. Strange flipped the Zealot away, directly into the rain forest behind him.

Before the Zealot knew what was happening, Strange's hand was already on the control dial. With a spin, the rain forest was gone, and in its place was a sunlit view of a vast, rocky, wide-open canyon.

"Two down, one to go."

Strange straightened himself, whirling around in the opposite direction. Kaecilius was waiting for him.

CHAPTER

12

How long had Strange been waiting? Had it been days, weeks, months...years since the accident? Time had become a meaningless concept for Strange.

Only time will tell.

How long had Strange been waiting for his miracle? To find the one thing that could restore hope and meaning to his life? To find the one thing that had restored hope and meaning to Jonathan Pangborn's life? To find Kamar-Taj?

A chill wind caught Strange in the face, and he did his best to pull the collar of his threadbare coat closer to his cheeks. It didn't work. Since he had arrived in Nepal, he had experienced cold like he had never experienced before. This was a world away from New York City, and all that he was used to.

Away from the hospital and the accident.

Away from Christine.

Strange continued to walk, as he had been doing for days (weeks?), as he arrived at the outskirts of the city of Kathmandu. It was bustling with activity. Cars, trucks, and people on bicycles and scooters weaved in and out of the foot traffic on the busy street.

He looked around and noted the odd blend of ancient-looking buildings, which almost all looked like temples or shrines, and the brightly painted modern structures beside them. Men and women sat by the side of the road, barely noticing the bedraggled, dirty figure walking among them.

Strange adjusted the backpack that hung on his weary shoulders. It felt heavy, even though there was very little in it. All of Strange's worldly goods had been sold or traded away in an effort to find his way here. No, not here, to Kathmandu. To Kamar-Taj.

The things that were his hands throbbed. They always throbbed. Since the accident, there had been nothing but pain. Nothing. Strange glanced down at the dirty, tattered bandages and frowned.

Continuing on his path, Strange passed through a crowded alleyway. He had come this far, and yet, he still didn't know where exactly he was headed. He had found the haystack. Now he had to find the needle.

He would need a miracle to find his miracle.

Looking around, Strange had to chuckle as he looked at the buildings, many of which bore signs in English.

"'Himalayan Healing. Find Peace. Find Yourself,'" Strange read aloud. "'Enlightenment Spa and Massage.' 'Chakra Bar.' 'Holy Tours.'"

He might as well have been in New York. All these businesses catered to tourists, to people who were seeking inner peace or a truth that eluded them. Strange shook his head. This was not the needle in a haystack he was looking for.

Moving on, Strange came upon a huge temple, swarming with local villagers. He saw people kneeling in prayer, spinning wheels devoted to their religion. Without even thinking, Strange extended a bandaged extremity toward one of the prayer wheels and gave it an absentminded spin.

Ahead of him, a line of tourists waited to receive blessings from an elderly monk.

He let out a heavy sigh.

"Kamar-Taj? Excuse me, do you know where I can find Kamar-Taj?" Strange asked a local, who didn't give the man with the scraggly beard a first look, let alone a second.

If Strange hadn't been so caught up in trying to find someone to direct him to Kamar-Taj, he might have noticed the presence of a hooded figure lurking in the shadows, his back to Strange. The man tilted his head slightly, as if listening to Strange. He wore a green robe.

"Kamar-Taj?" said a child, who limped toward Strange. The child hobbled along on a lone crutch, regarding Strange with a mixture of curiosity and contempt.

"Yes!" Strange shouted. Then, hopefully, excitedly, he added, "You speak English?"

The child extended his hand toward Strange, palm up. "Kamar-Taj?"

Strange shrugged. "I'm broke, kid. I spent my last dollar just getting here."

"Kamar-Taj?"

Strange sighed. What he'd said wasn't exactly true. He *did* have some money left—a few dollars, barely anything. But he had come this far; what else could he do? He reached into his wallet, fumbled with his useless, bandaged digits, and then handed a bill to the child.

The child took the bill, shoved it in his pocket, and then pointed ahead with his finger. Strange looked in that direction, then back at the child.

"A thousand rupees for you to point east? Thanks, beggar kid."

"You beggar, not me," the child shot back. Strange smiled. So the kid *could* speak English, after all.

"Yeah, okay," Strange said, still smiling.

The child laughed. "Patan Durbar Square."

"Patan Durbar Square?" Strange repeated.

The child nodded as he hobbled away into the flood of people. Strange started in the direction of Patan Durbar Square.

The man in the green robe followed.

Patan Durbar Square was teeming with palaces and temples. Strange walked through the complex. He was here. One step closer to finding the needle.

An unfamiliar feeling came over Strange, an eerie sensation like he was being watched. He looked around, but saw no one immediately near him, nothing to indicate danger.

That's when Strange noticed the man in the green robe staring at him. He tried to ignore the feeling, but eventually he looked back, only to find that the man in the green robe was no longer there. He shivered for a moment, then moved down a cobblestone alleyway. He *knew* he was close to finding Kamar-Taj, but it still seemed a world away.

As he stepped along the stones, a small dog limped toward Strange. It trailed one of its legs on the ground, broken. Strange looked at the dog, then resumed walking.

The dog started whining. Strange looked back at the dog.

"I've got a friend who goes for your type," he

said, thinking of Christine. She had tried to help Strange, help him through this living nightmare. And he had pushed her away. Why? What was he afraid of?

Walking back, Strange knelt down, and the dog approached him. His bandaged hands shaking, Strange gently examined the dog's leg. Definitely broken. But it could be fixed. He turned to his backpack and clumsily removed some of its pieces. With effort, he managed to tie a makeshift splint to the dog's leg. With time, the leg would heal.

It will heal, Strange thought sadly. *Only time will tell.*

As Strange picked the dog up and gently placed it on the stone street, the man in the green robe watched, tilting his head. Then he disappeared into the shadows.

Your watch," said a burly-looking man with a beard, stepping out of a doorway, blocking Strange's way. He practically spat the words at Strange. Strange looked around, the New Yorker in him realizing that he was in a tough spot. In addition to the bearded man, he saw another large man and a skinny guy approaching him.

"I don't have any money," Strange said reflexively. Then he realized he *was* wearing a watch. The watch that Christine had given him.

Only time will tell…

"No. Please. It's all I have left," Strange begged.

The bearded man wasn't taking no for an answer. "Your watch," he repeated, then shoved his hand out, waiting. Strange scrunched up his face, ready for a fight...not that he would be able to put up much of one. He desperately tried to cover his watch with his bandaged extremities, which made the bearded man laugh.

Ripping the backpack from his shoulder, the bearded man continued to laugh at Strange. The skinny guy slipped in, grabbing for the watch. Somehow, Strange evaded him, then ran—only to find the other large man in his way. They snared Strange in their arms. He struggled to free himself from their grasp, to hide the wrist with the watch.

They punched. They kicked. Strange groaned.

The skinny thief snatched the watch from Strange. But then the man in the green robe appeared.

Strange wasn't quite sure what happened next. It occurred so fast, it was basically a blur. Time seemed to speed up.

He saw hands and feet and punches and kicks flowing from the man in the green hood. He saw the bearded man, the large man, and the skinny guy falling to the ground and hitting the pavement, and then picking themselves up and running away.

Amazed, Strange fought to regain his senses as he saw the man in the green robe slowly remove his hood. The face that stared back at him was not kind. It had a particular menace to it, something that Strange couldn't quite name. The face had scars, from what he could not guess.

The man in the green robe stared at Strange, lying in the dirt. Strange picked himself up, breathing hard, and said, "My watch."

The man in the green robe moved his hands slowly, producing the watch—he had taken it back from the thieves. He looked at the watch, then threw it to Strange. Strange fumbled to catch the watch with his bandaged hands.

The watch was broken. The glass had cracked. It wasn't ticking.

Only time will tell, Strange thought.

At last, the man in the green robe spoke. "Sadly, I wasn't in time to save your bracelet."

"It's a watch," Strange muttered.

"Not anymore."

Strange stared in silence. After a while, the man in the green robe spoke again.

"You said you were looking for Kamar-Taj."

CHAPTER

13

Kaecilius was looking right at Stephen Strange when he knocked "Mister Doctor" onto his back. In a flash, he was all over Strange, energy forming around his hands, crackling.

Strange was dazed. Nowhere near as dazed as he had been the first time he encountered The Ancient One, but still dazed. He saw a nearby vase, then kicked out his leg, sending the vase toward Kaecilius. The vase crashed into the Zealot, knocking him off-balance.

An opening.

Strange got up and ran down the hallway, which was once again a regular hallway. Kaecilius had recovered and was right behind him. Strange ran into the room of relics that he had visited just moments ago. (Had it been just moments ago?)

The Chamber of Relics greeted Strange, and he leveled his gaze at an object he recognized almost immediately.

"The Brazier of Bom'Galiath!" he said, grabbing it. He recognized the object from his studies at Kamar-Taj. Turning around, he saw Kaecilius smirking.

"You don't know how to use that, do you?" said Kaecilius.

Strange stared at his foe, thinking.

No. No, he didn't.

Kaecilius advanced.

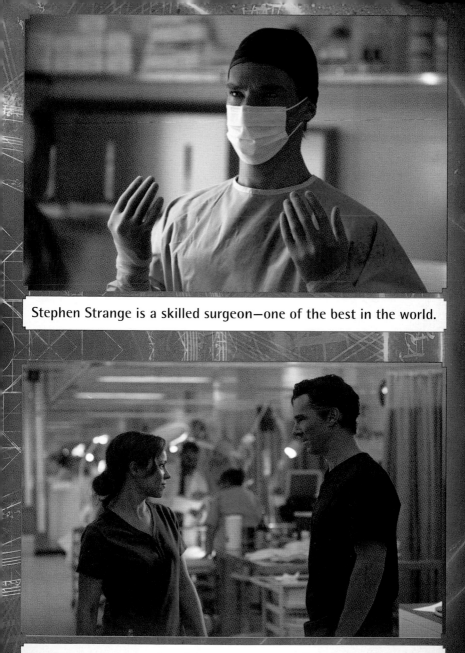

Stephen Strange is a skilled surgeon—one of the best in the world.

Christine Palmer works with him at the hospital. Their relationship is complicated, in part because of Stephen's arrogance.

After a horrible accident, Stephen is no longer able to perform surgery. His hands tremble when before, they moved with grace and precision.

He travels across the world to Nepal to find a cure for his injuries and crosses paths with a man known as Mordo.

Mordo takes Stephen to Kamar-Taj, a city known for its miracles, and introduces him to The Ancient One.

She is a mystic with great power.

The Ancient One shows Stephen that everything he thinks he knows about the nature of the universe is a mere layer in the greater Multiverse.

His mind opened to possibilities, Stephen trains in the mystic arts, both physically with Mordo...

...and mentally with Wong.

He soon learns of a great threat: Kaecilius and his followers.

Formerly pupils of The Ancient One, these zealots are in search of even greater and more dangerous knowledge than she was willing to teach.

On the cusp of their first battle, Stephen is thrust through a portal that takes him to the Sanctum Sanctorum in New York City.

Here, he must accept his role and use all his training to overcome Kaecilius's attack and fulfill his destiny as Doctor Strange, the Sorcerer Supreme!

Strange threw the Brazier of Bom'Galiath at him as hard as he could.

Kaecilius ducked.

It was worth a shot, Strange thought.

Kaecilius was upon him once more, and the two grappled. Appropriately for a fight in a room of relics, Kaecilius had produced a scythe, although Strange wasn't exactly sure how, and he now slashed at Strange with the weapon. He knocked the doctor to the floor, then advanced once again. A kick of inhuman strength sent Strange flying through a glass case full of relics, which shattered, scattering its contents across the room.

Kaecilius then threw Strange against another glass case, containing a cloak of the deepest red, shattering its glass as well. As Kaecilius prepared to strike Strange again with his scythe, a curious thing happened.

The cloak, finding itself freed from its glass enclosure, came to life.

It wrapped itself around Stephen Strange.

It deflected Kaecilius's blows.

Strange smiled.

CHAPTER

14

Strange found himself walking down another narrow alley. There was silence. And there was the man in the green robe, who walked beside him. The alley seemed almost impossibly narrow, and yet the two men managed to navigate through it just fine.

Emerging from the alley, the pair approached what appeared to be an ancient temple. Almost secreted in the stone alcoves that dotted the way were men with long beards and painted faces. Holy men, Strange guessed. He stopped, and was surprised to see the man in the green robe keep walking.

This isn't Kamar-Taj? Strange thought.

The man in the green robe bypassed the ancient temple and came to a plain, simple wooden door that definitely was not part of the temple.

Strange was confused.

"You sure you have the right place?" Strange said, pointing back at the temple. "That one looks a little more Kamar-Taj-y."

The man in the green robe stared at Strange, their eyes meeting uncomfortably.

"I once stood in your place," said the man in the green robe. "And I, too, was disrespectful. So might I offer a piece of advice?"

Strange gulped, then nodded.

"Forget everything you think you know."

Inside the door, Strange found another world. The building seemed so small on the outside, and yet the courtyard he now saw contained multitudes. There were various ceremonial courtyards, and people everywhere—it was like a city unto itself. Strange saw men and women wearing robes, engaging in all manner of activity. Some were meditating. Some were practicing martial arts. He heard chanting in languages he didn't recognize.

And yet, as he looked closer, he saw that some people were wearing sneakers and sunglasses.

Someone was listening to music through earbuds. Another person clutched a group of scrolls under one arm and cradled a small tablet computer in the other.

Forget everything you think you know, indeed, Strange thought.

Inside the complex, the man in the green robe guided Strange to an ornate structure. He stopped, then gestured.

"The sanctuary of our teacher," he said, "The Ancient One."

Strange looked at his guide. "Really? 'The Ancient One'?" Instantly, Strange realized his gaffe, as the man in the green robe regarded him with distaste. "Right, forget everything I think I know. Sorry."

The man in the green robe led Strange into the sanctuary. The hall had a high ceiling, supported by stone columns. If ever there was a temple, this was it. As the pair walked into the sanctuary, Strange noted an old man with a long beard with his hands tucked inside his robe. Four women moved into the room. One took Strange's worn overcoat, and another motioned for him to sit. Still another arrived with a tray of tea, and the last woman poured the tea.

Silence.

Uncomfortable and anxious, Strange spoke. "Thank you for seeing me," he said to the old man.

"You're welcome," came the response. But the old man hadn't said a word.

It was the woman pouring the tea who had spoken. Surprised, Strange looked at the woman. She seemed ageless, young and old at the same time. She had no hair on her head, and was scarred, not unlike the man in the green robe.

The man in the green robe made a gesture. "The Ancient One."

"Thank you, Master Mordo," she said.

Mordo. So the man in the green robe had a name. Nodding, Mordo stepped back, as The Ancient One took in the man who was Stephen Strange.

"Mister Strange."

"Doctor, actually," he said.

The Ancient One smiled. "Not anymore, though, right? That's why you're here." With effort, Strange raised the cup of tea to his lips. As he did so, The Ancient One saw his bandages and the scars beneath. "You've undergone many procedures. Seven, from the looks of it." Strange was taken aback. How did she know?

"Did you heal a man named Pangborn?" he asked. "A paralyzed man?"

"In a way," The Ancient One responded. Strange became more anxious.

"You helped him to walk again. I was astonished! How could you have corrected a complete spinal-cord injury?" Strange asked.

The Ancient One smiled thinly at Strange. "I didn't correct it. He couldn't walk. I convinced him that he could."

"You're suggesting that his problem was psychosomatic—that it was in his head?" Strange asked in disbelief.

The Ancient One shook her head. She leaned in. "When you reattach a severed nerve, is it you that heals it back together, or the body?"

"It's the cells," Strange said, starting to get impatient.

"And the cells are only programmed to put themselves back together in very specific ways."

"Right," Strange said in a clipped tone.

"What if I told you," The Ancient One said with a lilt in her voice, "that your body can be convinced to put itself back together in all sorts of ways?"

Strange closed the gap between him and The Ancient One. "You're talking about cellular regeneration! Bleeding-edge medical tech. Is that why you're working here, without a governing medical board? Just how experimental is your treatment?"

The Ancient One stared at Strange, then gave Mordo a knowing look.

"Quite," she replied.

"So you've figured out how to reprogram nerve cells to heal themselves?"

"No, Mister Strange. I know how to reorient the spirit to better heal the body."

"The spirit heals the body," Strange echoed, unsure. The Ancient One nodded once more, and took a sip of tea. "Okay, how do we do that? Where do we start?"

Rising from her sitting position, The Ancient One walked across the room to an enormous book atop a table. She flipped through its pages, coming to one that showed a map of the human body, with seven chakras noted, along with a cluster of pressure points.

Strange had to laugh. "I've seen that before." He sneered. "In gift shops."

The Ancient One turned to another page.

Strange saw a similar map of the human body, this one detailing the nervous system.

"Perhaps you prefer this one?" She flipped through the pages again, and Strange saw an MRI image of the human body. "Or this one? Each of these maps was drawn by someone who could see in part, but not the whole," said The Ancient One.

Strange's mind raced; he felt disoriented. "I spent my last dollar getting here. And you talk of healing through belief. Let me tell you what I believe. Pangborn's injury couldn't have been complete. He must have had nerve fibers left!"

The Ancient One remained silent. Strange was now angry.

"So he had a spontaneous remission here? And you take the credit. Tell people it's your power. All they have to do is give up their worldly goods and join your little cult. Miracles for everyone!"

Mordo looked at The Ancient One, uncomfortable.

"No," said The Ancient One. "Not for everyone."

Strange shook his head in disgust. "Only the believers, right?"

"You're a man looking at the world through a keyhole," The Ancient One explained patiently. "And you've spent your whole life trying to widen that keyhole, to see more, to know more. And now, when hearing that it can be widened in ways you can't imagine, you reject the possibility."

That was the truth. But Strange still couldn't accept it.

"I reject it because I don't believe in fairy tales about chakras or energy or the power of belief!"

he thundered. "There's no such thing as spirit! We are made of matter, and nothing more."

The Ancient One chuckled. "You think too little of yourself."

"No, you think yourself too great," Strange said, his bandaged, scarred hands throbbing. "You're no different than I am! Just another tiny, momentary speck within an indifferent universe."

"And you judge the universe with paltry perception. And to the Multiverse, you are utterly blind."

"The Multiverse?" Strange replied, making no effort to hide his contempt.

"The reality you know is but one of many," The Ancient One said in response.

"Oh, really?" said Strange, sarcasm tingeing every word. "And where are they?"

"All around you," came The Ancient One's answer, matter-of-fact. "Everywhere and else-where, and sometimes nowhere at all. Free your mind...."

Strange could contain his anger no more. He rose, moving toward The Ancient One, wagging a bandaged finger accusingly.

"My god, this is all a big joke—a scam! Muggers take my wallet, and you 'magically' know my name! You think you see through me? Well, I... see...through...*you!*"

With that, Strange jabbed his finger at The Ancient One.

A mistake.

Before he could register what had happened, The Ancient One had grabbed Strange's hand, twisting it and stopping him dead in his tracks. The Ancient One moved aside, then took the palm of her hand and shoved it—not at all gently—into Strange's body.

Strange slumped. He dropped his teacup and it shattered on the floor. Mordo rushed to his side, catching Strange with one hand, holding him up.

Strange saw all of this, observed it like it was happening to someone else.

How...?

Strange looked at his hands. Like his body, they appeared translucent, luminous, glowing. He looked at Mordo and saw the man in the green robe holding his body. Wait, his body? Then what was *this*? What *was* he? What had he become?

Gesturing, The Ancient One motioned toward Strange. He felt displaced and disoriented, and found himself being held up by Mordo. He gasped for air and rose to his feet.

"What," he said, shaking, "did you just do to me?"

"I pushed your astral form out of your physical form."

Strange couldn't process this. He looked at the broken teacup on the floor, and the tea that had spilled from it.

"What's in the tea? Did you drug me?"

The Ancient One shook her head. "It's just tea," she said. "With a little honey."

"What...just...happened?" Strange asked.

"For a moment, you entered the Astral Dimension. A place where the soul exists apart from the body. For we are more than the measure of our matter."

Strange was in a daze. This was all too much. How could he have expected this? He stumbled backward, afraid. He knocked over a table. He had to get out of here, had to leave. The Ancient One watched Strange in his fit of panic, and from somewhere produced what looked like small metal knuckles. She slipped them over two fingers, and then, with a gesture, made reality give way.

Strange now found himself confronted with a mirror image of the room around them, but it was gray, dull, and lifeless. But when he saw himself and The Ancient One in the reflection, they were in color.

What on earth was happening?

"You are now inside the Mirror Dimension," The Ancient One explained. "Ever-present, but undetected, a reflection of reality as we know it."

As The Ancient One spoke, Strange found his already tenuous grip on reality slipping even further. The very walls of the room seemed to melt, to warp. Strange did not want to look, but he couldn't help himself. He turned to see Mordo and the women in the sanctuary, moving around, taking no heed as reality melted away.

"In the Mirror Dimension, space and matter can be folded without affecting or changing the real world. Using this dimension, we make gateways to travel great distances in an instant."

Strange stared agape as the room continued to melt and re-form itself. Up was down, and down was up; the floor was now the ceiling, and the ceiling became the floor. Strange looked up to see the women cleaning up the tea service. They paid him no heed.

Strange could not get his bearings, and he stumbled. He was like an infant taking his first steps, unsure and wobbling. He backed into the mirror image and then reality returned; everything was as it had been. Strange was sweating profusely, his heart racing. He couldn't breathe. He looked at The Ancient One.

"Why...are you doing this?"

"To show you just how much you *don't* know."

With that, The Ancient One placed a thumb upon Strange's forehead.

"Open your eye."

The floor fell away beneath Stephen Strange's feet, and he slid down as if it were a sheer wall. He kicked, he grabbed, and he screamed, to no avail. He slid down the floor (wall?) all the way to the far wall (floor?). There was a window.

He crashed right through it. He thought he was

dead and was shocked when he opened his eyes to see stars, blackness, and swirling colors he had never thought possible before.

Outer space.

He moved through the void with unimagined speed, his body a projectile careening through the universe. Passing stars, planets, nebulae, Strange's body was not his own as he hurtled along.

"This isn't real! This isn't real! This isn't real!" he screamed.

Below him, he saw Earth.

CHAPTER 15

In front of him, Strange saw Kaecilius. All around, the Chamber of Relics—the Sanctum Sanctorum itself—seemed to react to his presence in some intangible way, almost as if the building itself could sense the evil radiating from Kaecilius.

Kaecilius looked at Strange, who had the red cloak wrapped around him. If Strange didn't know any better, he would have sworn that Kaecilius smiled just a bit. Did he know something that Strange didn't?

Energy began to coalesce and throb around Kaecilius.

Strange's hands throbbed. *Not now*, he thought, pushing past the pain. He could literally feel the onslaught coming; the hairs on his arms stood straight up.

"Let's end this," Kaecilius said with a snarl.

CHAPTER

16

"K amar-Taj is not an end unto itself," said Mordo, "but a beginning." Strange walked beside Mordo through Kamar-Taj, toward a row of simple-looking rooms, listening.

"I gathered that, after falling through outer space," Strange replied dryly. He looked at Mordo with a weak smile.

Mordo glared.

At last, they came to one particular door, and

inside, Strange could see an unadorned room with a cot, a chest for belongings (as if he had any), a desk, and a book. Mordo raised his hand and pointed into the room.

"Bathe. Rest. Meditate, if you can," he said. "The Ancient One will send for you."

Strange gathered himself and walked into the room as Mordo handed him a small card. Looking down, Strange saw one word scrawled in elaborate handwriting:

SHAMBALLA

"What's this?" Strange asked. "My mantra?"

"Wi-Fi password," Mordo responded, deadpan. "We're not savages." Mordo turned and left the room, and Strange was at last alone with his thoughts. He walked over to the desk and looked at the book. It was bound in leather, and obviously very old. He flipped open the cover and couldn't suppress a laugh when he saw a tablet computer inside—the "book" was just a cover.

They are most definitely not *savages*, Strange thought.

There was a small window off to one side, and Strange walked over to it. Taking the watch off his wrist, he looked once more at the inscription on its back.

" 'Time will tell how much I love you,' " he said softly, reading the inscription. "Time will tell."

He thought of Christine and set the watch down on the windowsill.

The sun shone through the Kamar-Taj central compound, and there was an absolute feeling of spring in the air. With it, Strange was sure he could also feel something he had not felt in a very long time: hope.

After months spent traveling in the same shabby shirt and pants, Strange at last had a change of clothes. He now wore a gray uniform of tunic and pants. Mordo explained to him that gray was the color of the novice—a person just learning the ways of Kamar-Taj. It had been a long time since Stephen Strange had been a novice at anything.

Perhaps it was time to be a novice again.

As he walked through the central compound, Strange saw an enormous, ancient, gnarled tree. Dark-blue flowers bloomed from its branches, and Strange noted their beauty. It had also been a long time since he had noticed the beauty of a flower.

Strange could hear his footsteps echo as he walked into The Ancient One's sanctuary. She had sent for him, and he entered anxiously. He wanted to learn everything he could all at once, but he knew that wasn't possible. What he was about to do would require otherworldly patience.

The Ancient One sat on the floor, behind a low table. She looked very much at peace. Strange approached, uncertain. Lowering himself, Strange sat down directly across from her. The Ancient One noticed, but did not look at Strange. Instead, she picked up a brush that was resting on the table and dipped it in an inkwell. Turning to a piece of paper, The Ancient One painted what looked like a rune. The strokes were graceful, masterful, and The Ancient One's hand moved like a spring breeze.

"The language of the mystic arts is as old as civilization," she said, still not looking at Strange.

"Sorcerers of old called the use of this language *spells*."

Strange said nothing, shifting in his seat.

"If that word offends your modern sensibilities, call it a program. The source code that shapes reality," The Ancient One intoned. "We begin with a word."

She set the brush down on the table, then turned her eyes to focus on the rune she had painted.

"With the word, we focus our thoughts."

After what seemed like an eternity, The Ancient One raised her head, her eyes meeting Strange's.

"With thoughts, we focus the body."

Silently, The Ancient One performed a series of gestures with her hand, slicing through the air. Such precision, such grace. It was like watching a martial artist at work. The hand motions were so assured, so powerful, and yet so utterly beautiful.

"With the body, we harness the spirit."

She moved her hand once more, but this time The Ancient One's fingers left a luminous trail in the air itself. She was writing runes with her hand.

"And we make our intentions real."

When she was finished, Strange saw a rune hanging in the space between himself and The Ancient One. He could feel power emanating from the rune. The rune illuminated their faces, and Strange felt a peculiar warmth. Simply put, he was stunned. The Ancient One then tapped the rune with a single finger, and it faded away into nothingness. That same hand now moved even faster in the air, and produced a series of illuminated runes.

"We harness energy drawn from other dimensions in the Multiverse."

Strange watched, slack-jawed, as The Ancient One thrust a palm forward. As she did, an intricate mandala of light formed, hanging in the air, as did the runes. The mandala was full of symbols Strange did not recognize, calligraphy of a language he could not read. The mandala pulsed with energy, throbbed.

Strange's hands also throbbed, but for once he did not notice.

"To cast spells, to conjure shields and weapons... to make *magic*."

Without a sound, darkness overwhelmed them. The only light was now provided by the mandala, which hung before them.

As if in response, a wind whipped through the sanctuary, ruffling Strange's hair and robes. The mandala continued to pulse with energy, and it hummed.

The humming grew louder. The Ancient One formed her hand into a fist.

The mandala disappeared, as if it had never

existed. Light returned to the sanctuary, and there was silence.

"Even if...even if my fingers could do that, I'd just be waving my hands," Strange said in disbelief. "How do I get from *here*...to *there*?"

The Ancient One looked at Strange's hands. "How did you ever come to reattach severed nerves, or put a human spine back together, bone by bone?" she asked.

Strange thought, then responded, "Study and practice. Years of it."

The Ancient One nodded at Strange, as if to say, *At last you begin to understand.*

From the top of the Kamar-Taj compound, there was a breathtaking view of Kathmandu, with the sun rising just above the snowcapped mountains, its light dancing along the roof-tops. Strange turned his attention away from this beauty to the task at hand. He was studying with dozens of other students. Mordo was among them, helping lead the class.

As The Ancient One had before, Mordo now moved his hands and body, as if performing an elaborate martial art. The other students moved their bodies in the same way, at the same time. Collectively, their hands traced the now-familiar luminous runes into the air around them. The runes were identical—the students were learning the language of magic.

A large man walked among the students, around them, between them, surveying their every move. He had the air of an instructor—and a stern one, at that. The large man had a shaved head, and his eyes watched, absorbing every detail. His voice cut through everything as he counted out the sequence of motions required to write the runes.

Strange watched the instructor, then looked at the other students, who were progressing well, making their runes just as The Ancient One had. It had been weeks since Strange saw her display and the mandala. Weeks since it began to dawn on him just how much he truly had to learn. And judging by his performance right now, he absolutely had a great deal to grasp.

He struggled to keep up with the others. Forming the same motions and shapes in the air was a struggle for him. His uncooperative hands, and his miserable fingers, simply couldn't do it. Pain seeped in from the edges, even though Strange did his best to push it out. He motioned with his hands before him and looked.

There were no runes.

Strange took a deep breath, and began again.

"Time will tell...."

It felt like he was training all day, every day, even into the nights. And that's exactly what he was doing. He needed a break. Whereas before Strange would have called down for his sports car and gone for a long drive, speeding along highways while blasting music, he now took his comfort in, of all things, a library.

But it was hard to think of the Narthex as just a library, Strange mused. It was a library, he thought, in the same way that a whale was a fish. Then Strange remembered that whales were mammals, not fish, and his whole analogy fell apart. But he didn't care.

Everything about the Narthex screamed magic. It was lined with old books, none of which existed outside Kamar-Taj. This was not the place to find the latest self-help book or page-turning crime thriller. This was a place of ancient knowledge.

As Strange moved through the library, he found a man behind a desk. It was the same man who had been instructing the runes class, the one who had barked out the count. Strange could tell, through the robes the man was wearing, that he was powerfully built. He had a definite *do not mess with me* vibe about him.

"Mister Strange," said the man.

"Uh, yes. But please, call me Stephen," he responded. "And you are...?"

"Wong."

"Just *Wong?*"

Wong glared at Strange.

"Or Aristotle?" Strange said, trying to lighten the mood.

Wong said nothing, but motioned to Strange to put the stack of books he was carrying down on the desk. Wong picked up each volume, saying nothing, but examined the bindings and pages to ensure that everything was in order. It was then that he noticed exactly what Strange had been reading.

Wong stared at Strange, stared at the gray robes he wore—the robes of a novice. Wong narrowed his eyes.

"You...finished all these?" he said.

Unsure of what was happening, Strange nodded. Barely a moment passed before Wong rose from his seat, then motioned for Strange to follow him. He led Strange through the Narthex, through the massive stacks of books, to a set of stone stairs.

They took the stairs, which led to shelves full of even more ancient, more mysterious tomes. Beyond these stacks, Strange saw a pedestal, on which sat a peculiar object. It looked...like an eye? Like a golden eye?

"This section," Wong began, grabbing Strange's attention away from the object, "is for disciples and masters only. But at my...discretion, others may use it."

Wong lifted a heavy book and handed it to Strange.

"You should start with *Maxim's Primer*," Wong said, referring to the book now in Strange's hands. "How's your Sanskrit?"

Strange thought for a moment. Sanskrit was a

very old language, still used in certain parts of the world. *Not in my world*, Strange thought.

"I'm fluent in online translating," Strange replied. Wong paid Strange no heed, and started to hand more books to the novice.

"Vedic and classical Sanskrit," Wong said. Strange looked around him and saw a row of books that caught his eye. Somehow, they looked older than the rest.

"What are those?" Strange said, jabbing a finger toward the books.

"The Ancient One's private collection."

Strange nodded. "So they are forbidden?"

Wong shook his head. "No knowledge is forbidden in Kamar-Taj. Only certain...practices."

Pulling a book from the shelf, Strange looked at the title: *The Book of Cagliostro*.

"But those books are far too advanced for

anyone other than the Sorcerer Supreme," Wong said flatly, almost dismissing Strange.

Flipping through the book, Strange immediately noticed that something was amiss.

"This one has pages missing."

"*The Book of Cagliostro*. Two rituals stolen by a former disciple," Wong said, drawing a long breath. "The zealot Kaecilius, just after he strung up the former librarian and relieved him of his head."

Strange's eyes went wide. Wong explained how Kaecilius and a group of followers, also Zealots, had been a cause of growing concern for The Ancient One.

"I am now the guardian of these books. So if a volume from this collection should be stolen again, I'd know it, and you would be dead before you ever left the compound."

Strange's eyes went wider. "What if it's just... overdue? Any late fees I should know about?" No reaction. "Maiming, perhaps? An amputation?" Strange continued, trying to elicit some kind of response from Wong.

No reaction.

"You know, people used to think I was funny."

"These people," said Wong, "did they work for you?"

Strange gulped. "Well. Thank you for the books. And the horrifying story. And the threat upon my life."

With that, Strange picked up the stack of books and left the Narthex. The night air was cool, and it was raining.

CHAPTER 17

The accident. Kamar-Taj. The Ancient One.

It all led Strange here, to the Sanctum Sanctorum, to this moment.

Kaecilius before him. Kaecilius the Zealot, the madman, the murderer. Stealer of secrets.

Kaecilius, who lunged at Strange with such venom and force that it threw The Ancient One's disciple out of the Chamber of Relics and down the staircase, toward the foyer. In a blur, the cloak that had been covering Strange moved as if it were alive, sentient, soaring with mind-boggling speed out of the Chamber of Relics.

The Zealot ran out of the Chamber of Relics and down the hallway, then stopped in his tracks at the top of the staircase. That's when he saw Stephen Strange, floating above the stairs, wrapped in the cloak.

"The Cloak of Levitation," Kaecilius said through gritted teeth. "Twelfth-century design by the weaver Enitharmon. Has a mind of its own."

Strange allowed a slight smile to play across his face. "I guess it likes me."

The Zealot raged at Strange, slashing. Before Strange could even react, the cloak yanked him backward with incredible speed. His heels dragged along the floor.

Now it was his turn. Once more, he summoned

a luminous whip to his hand, cracking it at Kaecilius. The Zealot flinched. The cloak then threw
itself (and Strange along with it) into Kaecilius.
Cloak, disciple, and Zealot plummeted to the
ground.

CHAPTER

I'm falling flat on my face.

That thought raced through Stephen Strange's mind as he trained atop the roof at Kamar-Taj once again. The morning sun beamed down on Strange and the other students. Mordo stood in front of them. He wore the now-familiar two-knuckled metallic object that Strange knew was called a sling ring. Strange and the other students wore sling rings on their hands as well.

Each student—except Strange—carved large

gateways in the air before them. The gateways glowed, luminous.

"Visualize," Mordo instructed. "See the destination in your mind. The clearer the picture, the quicker and easier the gateway will come." Mordo watched Strange as he struggled to form the gateway. He turned to see The Ancient One approaching him, along with the old man who often accompanied her. The man had his hands folded in his robes.

"I would like a moment alone with Mister Strange," said The Ancient One.

"Of course," Mordo replied. His face betrayed shame—shame that Strange appeared to be making no progress under Mordo's teaching. Mordo walked away, beckoning the other students to accompany him. The Ancient One and the old man sat down, facing Strange. Strange grimaced. He knew what was going on here.

He was falling. Failing.

"My hands—"

"It's not about your hands," The Ancient One interrupted.

Strange looked at The Ancient One, not believing what he was hearing. "How is this *not* about my hands?"

"Hamir," said The Ancient One, gesturing to the old man beside her.

In response, Hamir raised his arms, pulling them from his robes. He showed his hands to Strange. Or rather, his one hand. On the other arm, where the hand should be was a smooth stump, ending just above the wrist. Hamir stood a moment, then waved his stump in the air, trailing luminous writing in its wake.

Strange couldn't believe it. Even with a missing hand, Hamir was creating the runes. Hamir finished his display, then returned his arms to his robes. He bowed to The Ancient One, then turned and walked away.

The Ancient One gazed into Strange's eyes. "It's not about your hands. You cannot beat a river into submission. You have to surrender to its current and use its power as your own."

"I control it by surrendering control," Strange summarized. "That makes no sense."

"Not everything does. Not everything has to. Your intellect has taken you far in life, but it will take you no further," she said. "Surrender, Stephen. Silence your ego, and your power will rise."

He nodded as if he understood, but Strange was certain that he didn't. The Ancient One stood up, Strange along with her. With her sling ring, she cleaved a gateway into the air. She walked through, saying, "Come with me."

Strange followed.

Where was he? Atop a mountain. *Mount Everest?* They were high up, he and The Ancient One. Below them, Strange could see a valley. Above, he could see the summit of Everest, cresting into the sky.

"Beautiful," The Ancient One observed.

Strange nodded as he wrapped his arms around himself. "Freezing," Strange said through chattering teeth, "but beautiful."

"At this temperature the average person can last thirty-two minutes before suffering permanent loss of function. But you will likely go into shock within the first two."

Strange nodded again, and before he knew it, The Ancient One had stepped back through the gateway. He dove toward the gateway, but was too late—it had already closed. Strange was rewarded with a face full of snow as he landed on the ground.

"No, no, no, no, *no!*" Strange shouted.

He knew there was only one way off the mountain, only one way to avoid certain doom.

The sling ring. A gateway.

Strange slipped the sling ring onto his hand and began performing the gestures that would form the gateway.

Nothing.

Panic gripping him, Strange tried moving his hands faster.

Again, nothing.

A top the compound at Kamar-Taj, Mordo paced toward The Ancient One. His brow was furrowed.

"Perhaps I was wrong about him," Mordo said apprehensively.

"We shall see," The Ancient One offered. "Any minute now." Mordo looked at his master. Suddenly, he realized what The Ancient One had done with Strange, and where he now was.

"Not again," Mordo begged. This had happened before, with other students. It was a favorite test of The Ancient One's. She smiled at Mordo.

"Perhaps I should—"

The Ancient One shook her head. Mordo was not to lift one sling-ringed finger.

They waited.

Nothing.

Until there was something.

A gateway opened before them. From it, Stephen Strange emerged, shivering, covered in snow, teeth chattering. He couldn't take his eyes off The Ancient One. He was full of anger, and ready to unload on her, until it hit him: He had done it.

The things that had been his hands ... Strange had made them perform a miracle.

He felt hope.

The Ancient One smiled at him.

At night, Strange found himself in his chamber once more. Standing over the washbasin, he slowly cut away at his shaggy hair, returning it to a respectable length. Then he pulled out an anomalous electric razor and shaved his face. His fingers twitched and trembled, but he pressed on. He shaped the beard.

He looked into the mirror, at the things that... at the things that were his hands.

They trembled. But he had done it.

He had done it!

S trange stared out his window, and his eyes fell on the watch that still lay on the sill. He walked over and picked it up with his trembling fingers.

Time will tell...

He picked up the tablet computer that was on the small desk and opened his e-mail. Slowly, laboriously, he moved his twitching fingers over the keyboard and typed:

Christine, I know it's been

He deleted the line.

"How," he said out loud, "am I supposed to explain *this*?"

The air was crisp with the coming of fall, and Strange found himself once more atop the roof of the Kamar-Taj compound. He was with Mordo, training, as usual. Mordo had removed his shirt, revealing a quilt of scars and—were those bullet wounds? *What happened to Mordo?* Strange wondered. *What brought him here, to The Ancient One?*

"So no one really knows her name?"

"No one," Mordo said, lacing up his leather boots.

Strange tugged at his robes. The ones he wore now were red—the color of an apprentice. Strange had learned much in the days...weeks... months...since he'd arrived at Kamar-Taj.

"How ancient *is* she?" Strange asked.

Mordo looked at Strange and said, "Would you believe she was born from a Hebridean rowan tree over five thousand years ago?"

Strange recoiled from Mordo in disbelief. And yet maybe...

"From a tree? What does...? How can...?" Strange fumbled.

Mordo laughed loudly. "I'm kidding. Truth is, she was a hiker who came here ten years ago and never left."

"What...really?" Strange said, falling for it.

Mordo smiled. "Look at you, Doctor I-Don't-Believe-in-Fairy-Tales—ready now to believe anything I say!" Mordo chuckled. "Nobody knows the age of the Sorcerer Supreme, when she inherited the title, or from where exactly she hails. All I know is that she's Celtic, from traditions remembered now only by her. She simply is, and we are all the better for it."

As Strange absorbed his words, Mordo thrust a quarterstaff into his hands. The weapon crackled with tangible energy.

"What is this?" Strange asked.

"It's called a relic," said Mordo, readying himself. "The manipulation of dimensional energies puts a strain on our minds. Some magic is too powerful to sustain, so we imbue objects with it, allowing the object to take the strain we cannot."

In a flash, Mordo was on his feet, raising his own quarterstaff, facing Strange.

"This," Mordo said, motioning to his quarterstaff, "is the Staff of the Living Tribunal."

SMACK! The two began to spar, their staves cracking into each other, unleashing a torrent of sparks.

"Other relics include—"

SKRACK!

"—the Wand of Watoomb, the Pincers of Power, the Hoary—"

VRAACK!

"—Hosts of Hoggoth, the Crimson Bands of Cyttorak, the—"

Strange lowered his quarterstaff, laughing. He was practically doubled over.

"What?" asked Mordo, not in on the joke.

"Who names these things?"

Mordo pondered the question, throwing Strange a stern look. Then he shrugged. He didn't know.

"I haven't even mentioned the Brazier of Bom'Galiath yet."

SKRACK!

Once more, Strange and Mordo clashed in their practice battle. Mordo was big and fast, strong and agile, and he had the edge of experience. Who knew how long he had been studying under The Ancient One?

But Strange was a quick study. Slowly, he began to get the upper hand.

SKRRRIIIKKK!

Strange batted aside Mordo's quarterstaff with his own. He was winning. "Elizabeth!" Strange shouted.

"What?" Mordo asked, confused.

"She looks like an Elizabeth!"

Strange's confidence was mounting, enough to let his sense of humor creep in, just as it had done when he had faced difficult surgeries. But Mordo still had experience on his side. His boots began to glow, and suddenly, as Strange watched, helpless, Mordo vaulted over his head.

While Strange hesitated for only a second, Mordo took that moment to press his advantage. He slammed the end of the quarterstaff into Strange's body, sending him to the floor. Mordo swung the staff toward Strange's head, a killing blow.

He stopped an inch from Strange's face. "Fight like your life depends upon it, because one day, it may." Strange panted. He nodded. Mordo was right.

"And," Mordo added gravely, "she looks like a Catherine."

CHAPTER 19

Strange was fighting as if his life depended upon it.

It did. Mordo had been right.

There was punching, a flurry of blows thrown by both sides. Some landed, some didn't. Mostly, Strange's didn't. Kaecilius had set the rules for this game, and he was beating Strange. Through a haze, Strange saw an ax on the ground—a relic, he guessed. He reached for the ax, only to find the cloak pulling at him once more, away from the object of his salvation. What was the cloak thinking?

The cloak stopped pulling, and that's when Strange saw what it *wanted* him to see. Mordo had mentioned them in passing; Wong had talked about them. Strange recognized them from all the reading he had done in those late nights at the Narthex.

The Crimson Bands of Cyttorak.

Strange threw them at Kaecilius. Snarling, Kaecilius tried to duck the Bands, without success. Quickly, the Bands wrapped themselves around Kaecilius, shackling his arms, his waist, his body, his mouth—binding him to the floor. He struggled.

"The Crimson Bands of Cyttorak," Strange said. "Forged by the smithies of Babylon three thousand years ago. Strong stuff."

A hush fell over the Sanctum. For the first time since Kaecilius had arrived, all was quiet. Strange looked at his fallen foe, then, with a gesture of his hand, removed the shackle from the Zealot's mouth.

Kaecilius began to chant, but Strange didn't recognize what he was saying.

"Stop it," Strange commanded. The Zealot didn't. "I said stop it."

"You cannot stop this, Mister Doctor...." Kaecilius sneered.

The Cloak of Levitation fluttered around Strange as he circled Kaecilius. "I've *already* stopped you, and I don't even know what 'this' is."

Kaecilius looked at Strange as if he were a child—unknowing. "It is the end *and* the beginning. The many becoming the few becoming the One."

"Look, if you're not going to make sense, I'm just going to have to put the muzzle back on," Strange said, brandishing his hand.

"Tell me, Mister Doctor—"

Strange let out a heavy sigh. "Okay, let me at least get one thing to make sense. The name is Doctor Stephen Strange."

"You're a doctor. A scientist. You know the laws of nature. All things age. All things die. In the end, our sun burns out. Our universe grows cold and perishes. But the Dark Dimension, it is a place beyond time."

The Dark Dimension.

Strange felt a gnawing fear grip his mind, an unsettling feeling that made his senses scream.

CHAPTER

20

He was wearing the blue tunic and pants, the robes of a disciple of The Ancient One. A sling ring dangled from his belt. It was a cold December day. It was raining, and the drops beat down upon Stephen Strange's forehead.

Drop. Drop. Drop.

Time will tell....

Water, cold. *My hands?*

As was now the norm, he carried a thick stack of books across the courtyard. He passed the ancient tree, the one whose blue flowers had been so welcoming in spring. The tree was now barren, its vital essence locked for the winter.

He headed for the Narthex.

Strange took a bite of an apple, the crunching sound penetrating the stillness of the library. He made an *oops!* face, and looked around to see if he was disturbing anyone. Like Wong. Especially Wong. He was surrounded by a stack of books, sprawled out on a table around him.

He flipped through the pages of *The Book of Cagliostro*. Something on one of the pages caught his eye. Rather, *it* was an eye, or it looked like one, anyway. There was a drawing of an amulet.

Beneath it, Strange read the descriptor: *The Eye of Agamotto*.

He looked up and saw Mordo. And Wong.

They were looking at him as if he had done something wrong. Had he? Immediately, Strange felt the need to apologize.

"I have a photographic memory. It's how I earned an MD and a PhD at the same time," he started. Mordo and Wong stared at Strange in disbelief. Had he *really* read all those books? And understood them?

"You were born for the mystic arts," Mordo said. There was admiration in his voice, but something else, too. *Envy?*

"And yet my hands still shake," Strange said quietly.

"For now, yes," Wong said solemnly.

"Not forever?"

"How should we know, Strange?" Mordo sighed. "We're not prophets."

"Then what *are* we?" asked Stephen Strange.

Mordo looked at Wong, Wong at Mordo. "He's ready," Wong finally said. He clicked a nearby pedestal, and suddenly the ceiling came to life with light. There appeared a luminous map running the length of the ceiling. Strange looked up in wonder.

Taking a deep breath, Wong motioned at the three of them. "The true purpose of a sorcerer is to safeguard this world against other-dimensional threats." Three cities on the map began to glow. Entranced by the map, Strange continued to gaze toward it while Wong and Mordo did the same to Strange.

"Kamar-Taj is bound to three Sanctum Sanctorums, each guarded by its own master. Secret, holy places where the world's meridians of power intersect. The first Sorcerer Supreme, Agamotto, united these lines of energy." At those words, lines began to illuminate on the map above.

Wong continued, "He created the Constant, and it is the Constant that keeps us safe from extra-dimensional forces. The yellow lines represent the protective ley lines. The purple dots are the Sanctum Sanctorums."

Strange nodded, taking a step closer.

"What would a red dot mean?"

Wong looked at Mordo. "That would be bad," Wong replied.

"*Uhhhhh* . . . how bad?" Strange asked.

A sinking feeling developed in all three men as they looked up at the map. There was a small red dot directly over London, home to a Sanctum Sanctorum.

There was terrible danger in London. The world was in terrible danger.

Mordo activated a gateway. It glowed, then opened.

A second later, a man whom Strange did not immediately recognize ran through the gate, his face a mask of blood and panic. This, Strange would find out later, was Sol Rama, the master of the London Sanctum Sanctorum. Before Wong and Mordo could help him, a shard of crackling energy flew through the gateway, spearing Sol Rama in the chest.

The man dropped face-first onto the floor of the Narthex. The doctor in Strange took over, and he rushed to Sol Rama's side. Kneeling beside the fallen master, Strange looked up at the gate.

He could see two people in robes. There was something wrong with their eyes. They were gesturing wildly. The Zealots Wong had mentioned. The ones who followed Kaecilius. Wong knelt down next to Sol Rama, across from Strange. His muscles looked coiled, as if he were ready to pounce.

Mordo waved his hands, summoning a weapon to his side. He ran toward the gateway.

Then came the explosion.

The room shook, and Strange was blown backward, through a gate.

At least, that's what Strange thought had happened.

He found himself inside an unfamiliar stone room, his ears ringing. He felt pain everywhere. Pain—he was used to that. He pushed himself up off the ground, wobbling on his feet, trying to regain his balance. Was he in shock? Maybe. He took several deep breaths: *inhale, exhale.*

He looked around and saw a gateway, now closed. The gateway back to Kamar-Taj.

Strange was cut off from Wong, Mordo, and The Ancient One. He was stranded here, wherever "here" was. The enemies of Kamar-Taj were on the move.

"Hello! Anyone else here?" Strange called out. No response.

There was a door, Strange noticed. He walked through it. He found himself inside a large foyer, then turned to the front door.

Strange drew in a deep breath as he opened the door and surveyed in his surroundings. There was no mistaking it—this was New York City's Greenwich Village. Bleecker Street, to be specific.

(Thanks, street sign.) The telltale brownstone apartment buildings and coffee shops were a familiar sight to Strange, who used to live in this place, the city that never sleeps.

How did I get here? Strange asked himself.

The Beginning